To Red,

Princess Allee

Savy Leiser

Princess Allee

Written by Savy Leiser

Illustrated by Brenda Clemente

*This book is dedicated to the memory of
Allee's namesake grandparents,
Al Dybas and Lee Leiser.
They never met her,
but surely would have loved her.*

Foreword

A *forever home* is exactly what it sounds like: a home you can live in forever, with a family that will always love you unconditionally. Unfortunately, many dogs struggle to find their forever homes. After experiencing abuse or neglect by previous owners, dogs can end up in shelters, in foster homes, or sometimes as strays. As these dogs roam from place to place, they all have one wish: to find a family that will love them forever.

The Furever Home Friends series presents the stories of real dogs who have lived such lives. Some of these dogs have found their forever homes, and some are still looking. For every dog in these books, there are thousands more waiting for someone to give them the family they deserve.

Allee is so happy that you decided to welcome her into your heart. She can't wait to be your new Friend Furever.

You can call me Princess Allee.

That's because my name is Allee,
and I've decided I'm going to be a princess!

I'm going to live in a castle,
sit on a throne,
and wear a pink crown.

Pink brings out the shine in my black fur.

I don't live in a castle just yet.
I live in an animal shelter.

That's a place for dogs like me
who don't have homes.

Sometimes, volunteers
read us bedtime stories.

I like the princess stories the best!
The princesses are always so
glamorous
and *beautiful*
and *sassy*.

They remind me of myself.

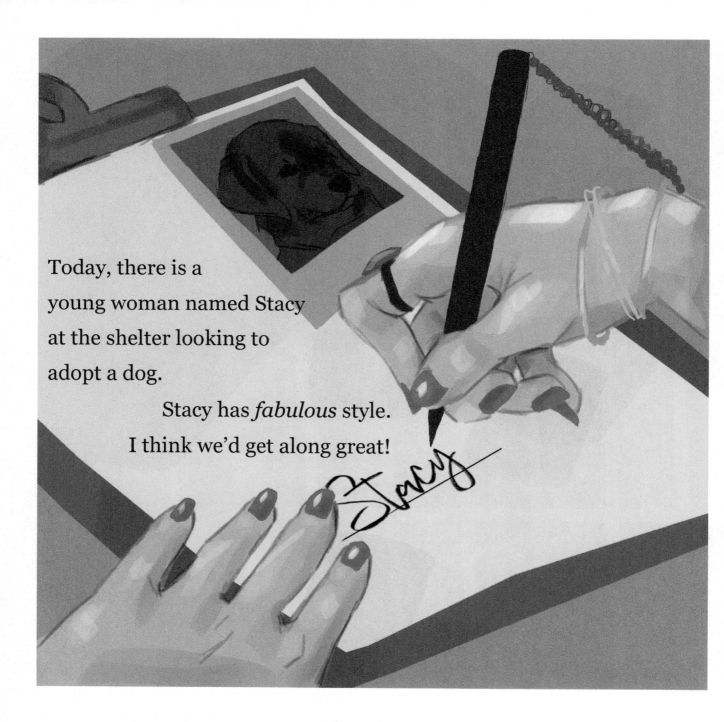

Today, there is a
young woman named Stacy
at the shelter looking to
adopt a dog.

Stacy has *fabulous* style.
I think we'd get along great!

"Allee, do you want to come live with me?" she says.

"I would treat you like a princess!"

Stacy *gets* me.

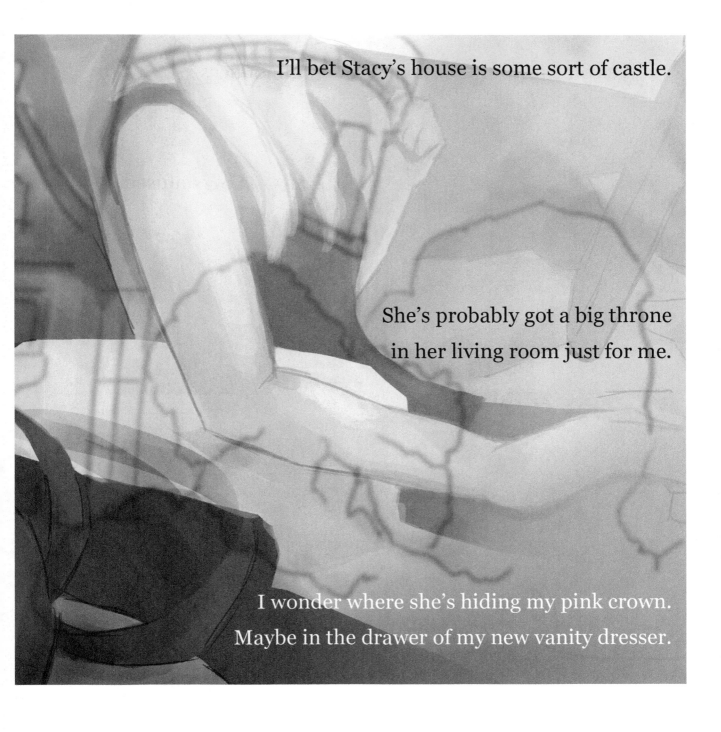

I'll bet Stacy's house is some sort of castle.

She's probably got a big throne
in her living room just for me.

I wonder where she's hiding my pink crown.
Maybe in the drawer of my new vanity dresser.

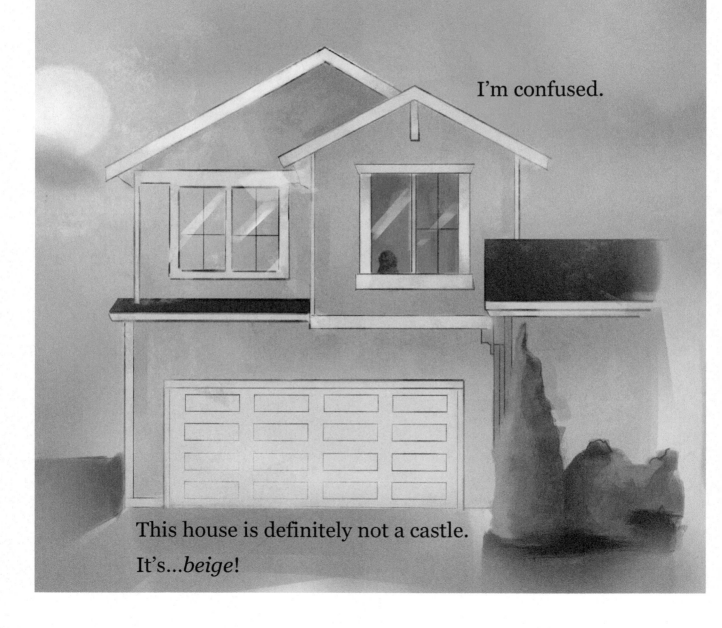

Inside, I don't see a throne anywhere!
Maybe this dog bed will do for now.

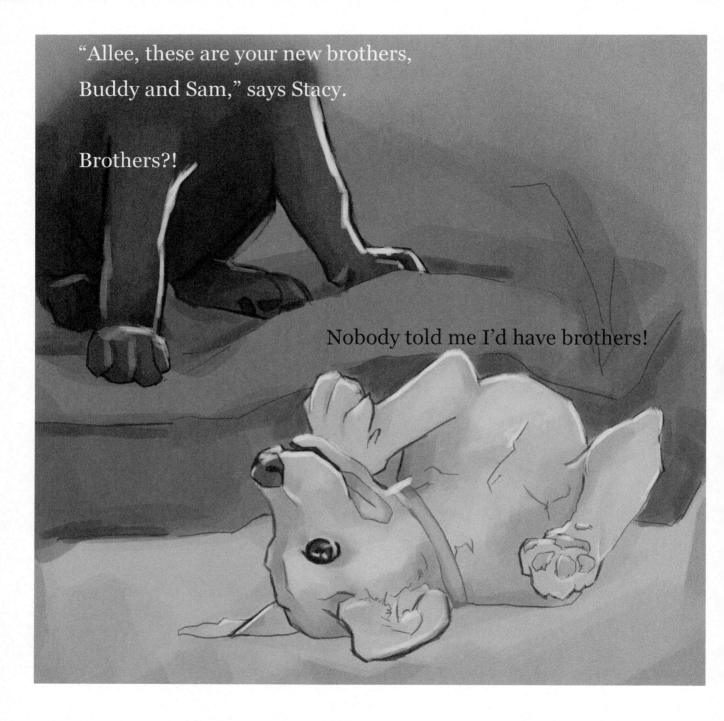

"Allee, these are your new brothers,
Buddy and Sam," says Stacy.

Brothers?!

Nobody told me I'd have brothers!

What kind of royal life *is* this, anyway?

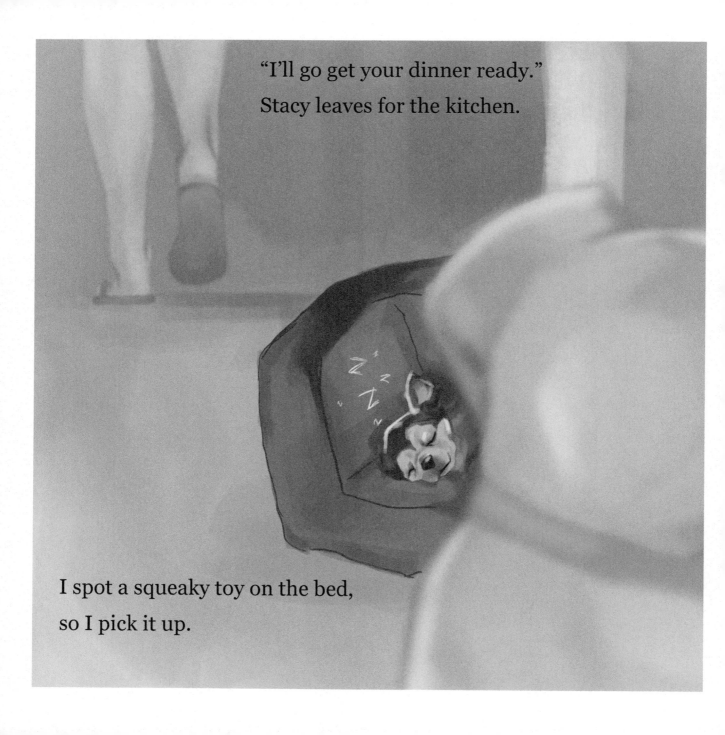

"I'll go get your dinner ready."
Stacy leaves for the kitchen.

I spot a squeaky toy on the bed,
so I pick it up.

"Let's play together!" Buddy excitedly barks.

"We can toss the toy back and forth!"

Buddy must not understand that
I'm supposed to be a *princess*.

That means I get at *least* this toy to myself.

Buddy lunges forward anyway and tries to
wrestle the toy out of my mouth.
It makes a loud *squeak*.
I pull back.
Squeak!
Buddy pulls again.

Squeak
SQUEAK
SQUEEEAK!

"What in the name of Lassie is going on here?" Sam barks.

Startled, Buddy and I drop the toy.

"You two are louder than fireworks on the Fourth of July! Can't Old Sammy ever get any peace and quiet around here?"

Buddy leans in to whisper in my ear.

"Sam's much older than we are.
He won't put up with any shenanigans from us."

I start giggling. *Shenanigans* is a funny word.

Buddy laughs along with me.

Next thing I know, Buddy and I have
lost ourselves in a fit of laughter.

That's when it hits me.

Buddy might not be fancy or glamorous...but he's fun.

Maybe playing with him could be fun too.

Buddy and I play and play and play.

We don't stop playing together until
Stacy returns from the kitchen with our food.

Stacy sets down three bowls of dog food.
She pats Buddy and Sam each on the head,
and then kneels in front of me.

"Allee, I'm so happy you became part of our family," she says.

"Oh, I almost forgot something!"

She rushes out of the room.

Stacy comes back holding a bright pink collar.

"I thought you might like this."

Today, I realized something important.

Stacy's house is better than any castle.

My new collar is better than any crown.

And Stacy, Buddy, and Sam

are better than any royal family.

Having a family that loves me

makes me feel like a princess!

Plus, the stones in this collar really bring out the sparkle in my eyes, don't you think?

Allee's Discussion Questions

for Kids, Parents, and Dogs!

1) At first, Allee wants to be a princess because she admires the princesses in her favorite stories. Who are some book characters you admire, and why?

2) When Allee gets adopted, she thinks she's going to live in a castle. Her new home does not meet her *expectations*, meaning it's different than she imagined it would be. When is a time something didn't meet your expectations? How did you make the best of that situation?

3) Allee doesn't get along with her new dog brothers right away. What are some difficulties siblings can face when trying to get along? How can they resolve them?

4) Allee and Buddy stop fighting over the toy when they start laughing together over the silly word *shenanigans*. Have you ever used humor to fix a problem?

5) At the end, even though Allee doesn't live in a castle, she still feels like a princess because her family loves her so much. What are some non-material things that make you feel special?

 Meet Allee

in Real Life!

Allee, Buddy, & Sam: 2007

Allee & Wrigley: 2017

Allee is a black lab living in Glenview, IL. She was adopted from a shelter in early 2007, when she was a puppy. She and her big brother Buddy were best friends for ten years, before Buddy passed away in early 2017 at the age of twelve.

Her big brother Sam—also a rescue dog—was born circa 1993, and passed away in 2008, when he was around fifteen years old. (Sam's definite birth year is unknown.)

Allee is now a wonderful big sister to Wrigley, another rescue dog. Wrigley plays with Allee all day until dinnertime, just like Buddy used to.

About the Author

Savy Leiser is a Chicago author, journalist, and freelance editor. In February 2016, Savy released her first young-adult novel, *The Making of a Small-Town Beauty King*. Savy earned her Bachelor's Degree from Northwestern University in 2015, and remains a devoted Wildcats fan. Outside of writing the *Furever Home Friends* series and working on new young-adult novels, Savy writes for *Halftime Magazine* and teaches creative writing workshops at Open Books.

You can visit Savy online at savyleiser.com.

About the Illustrator

Brenda Clemente is attending The Rhode Island School of Design for film, animation, and video, though she is an illustrator at heart. *Princess Allee* is her first children's book. You can find Brenda's other published work on the cover and interior of *The New Old Stock* magazine, issue 2. Before pursuing an art-related career, Brenda was a child caretaker who encouraged artistic expression with her employer's children. This project has reflected a wonderful fuse of her artistic interests while taking part in narratives that will bring joy to children's lives. This edition's artwork is dedicated to Charlotte, a tiny muse.

You can visit Brenda online at tassoartbc.wixsite.com/portfolio.

Acknowledgments

The Furever Home Friends would like to thank the following people for making this project possible:

ALIVE Rescue
The Anti-Cruelty
Society
Open Books
Jeff & Dolores Leiser
Steve & Terri Stewart
Tyler Stewart
Red Lhota
Emily Elliff
Sue Poppenhouse
Carol Williams
Heather Tennant
Angela Philipps
Carol DeMarco
The Fegley Family
Amy Ostrowski
Sabrina Townsend
Patty Byrnes
Christy Marie
Lois A. Leiser
Ryan Lauth
Jodi Murphy
Dr. Robin Newman
Sue Baumeister
Tom Saxton
Korina Dabundo
David Gottsegen
Jennifer Fulton

Westin Madix Hahn
Ben Francis
Madalyn Gisch
Lori Bowman
Sarah Grabinski
The Gehrig Family
Olivia Leiser
A. Rayburn, in
Memory of Betsy
Andrea Harding
Jon Davis
Jan Tennant
Jessica Stahmer
Polina Senderova
Gabe Watson
The Westlake Pack
Teresa Groat
Austin Pickrell
Kathy
Giannakopoulos
Molly Grace
Robyn Latchford
Aunt DC & Uncle Don
Aaron Kornick
Debbie Douglas, in
Memory of Gunney
Meghan Willard
Andrew Rogers

Deanne Ross
Glen Burkhardt
Alec Sumner
Clifford & Daisy
Ammons
Urania Smith
Regan Zehr Taylor
Jon & Chewy Drake
Liz Bell
Alex Gough
Gabi Carr
Natalie Stabrawa
Markie M.
Jordan Scherer
Megan Wines
Barrett Leider
Karl Maher
Aaron Graunke
Zach Luttmer
Samantha Bowen
Megan M. Miller
Sheila Welch
Luke Muller
The Holmes Family
Kali Maginity
Colleen
Lauren Scalzo
Lorraine Hughes

Aimee Hechler
James O'Rourke
Miles Hendrix
Hannah Nicolet
Stephanie Duchneskie
Anny Rusk
Jackie Elder
Irene Hechler
Janice Johnson
Gigi & Ryan Giles
Tara McManus
Corbin
Carla Dabundo
Cary Knox
Alexandria Paul
Carrie Dunfee
Michelle Pritchett
John David Buell
Marjorie Grenon
Brian Hajik
William Guenette
Joyce Strickland
Patrick Metcalf
Jim & Debbie
Glemkowski

Louisa Leiser
Starr Craft
Nancy Hatcher
Claire Grabinski
Brian Lasman
Tessa Weil
AJ Strauman
Antonette Bitonti
Phelps
Isabel Abbott
Taylor Dilbeck
The Silverman Family
Isaac Dansicker
Allison Valentijn
Karin Nihls & Bill
Leiser
Drayton Alan
Lucinda Prosterman
Neeraj Chandra
Rachel Bussom
Leo Putnam
ErikaGrace Davies
Terran Empire
Publishing
Adam Julian

Alec Ziff
Dandan Mirembe
Chen
Erica Bizub
Grace Gabel
Victoria Pettis
Joshua Hiew
Cody Zervas
Lesley Jones
Derek Savage
Alex Kohanski
Ellen Barry
Jason Yoon
DNAinfo Chicago
Good Dog in a Box
Candace Robinson of
Literary Dust
Krissy Belden of
Krissy's Book Nook
The Unionville Times
My Puppy Club
Astro's Adventures
Book Club
Tammy Perlmutter

CPSIA information can be obtained
at www.ICGtesting.com
Printed in the USA
BVOW07*0151100817
491518BV00001B/2/P